Bad Billionaire

This text was originally published in India on the year of 2023.
The edits and layout of this version are Copyright © 2023
by Indrajeet Nayak

This publication has no affiliation with the original Author or publication company.

Bad Billionaire

Indrajeet Nayak

India
2023

CONTENTS

AMELIA

RON

AMELIA

RON

AMELIA

RON

AMELIA

RON

AMELIA

AMELIA

"I don't know why I let you talk me into it," I lamented to my best friend Callie on my cell phone.

She replied that one week's work could net one hundred thousand dollars-and it barely even counts as labor!

"Yes, but when I agreed to it it was just an idea. Now it is real and I must follow through," I stated.

"OK, AMELIA," Callie replied. "Remember what I said? All the man wants is an onstage engagement so his family won't put pressure on him and his old grandmother can believe he has found someone suitable before she passes on." That was all. No need for paying sex fees either - honestly he was smoking hot - just what you were looking for. You are going to spend an awesome week at an amazing hotel with good food and people you enjoy spending time with while also getting paid to do it all."

"You seem remorseful," I teased gently.

"Girl, you could handle this client, but I wouldn't trust you with another... messier one," Callie replied. "Now, though, I must leave. Don't forget you're only acting out a part like an actress would.

Callie cut off our call before I could respond, though I knew she was right. Perhaps the three bottles of wine we shared the previous evening had something to do with my decision to agree to her offer of being an escort; normally I was quite conventional and wasn't interested in dating for money; but Callie made being one sound quite attractive; maybe this deal could finally give me my freedom as an individual; after years of feeling pressured into trying on an image of perfection for too long this was finally my chance to let myself off and just be myself without anyone holding back; maybe this was my chance?

At five minutes before our meeting was to occur, I checked my watch again. This moment represented my last chance to back out if that were what I intended; yet I knew that was unlikely; one week and 100K without strings or sexual content would surely compel anyone. And who said there had to be any law saying they must use the term escort anyway?

"Miss Rogers?" I heard an inky male voice ask.

As soon as I took a deep, relaxing breath and turned around to look, my disappointment became overwhelming. The man behind me must have been around sixty and although he appeared clean and well groomed, he certainly wasn't my type at all.

But then I understood why this guy was paying for company, not because of no strings and no mess as Callie suggested, but because finding someone without strings wouldn't be easy - especially considering I could hear judgment from his family when introduced as AMELIA: My gold digger.

"That's me," I replied, hoping my voice sounded more cheerful than it felt. When he replied with, "Please come with me," my smile returned and my spirit lifted with every new step forward.

Your plane is almost ready for take-off - all we need now to load your luggage and seat you.

I followed him, pulling my suitcase behind. As we went along, he stopped briefly to accept it before following in close step with me. To keep from giving him side eye or becoming disappointed later, I forced myself to keep looking straight ahead without giving him side eyes of my own.

"Alfred!" exclaimed a female voice from behind us, and Alfred stopped walking immediately.

"Please excuse me," said he.

Unsure of what to do, I paused and waited.

"Once Miss Rogers is finished being helped, could you please go up to the second-floor lounge and take Ms Andrews' daughter down runway three?" asked a woman.

"Sure," he responded and we resumed walking together - giving me an immediate sense of relief.

"Do you work at the airport?" I inquired.

"Of course," Alfred replied with a smile, "otherwise why would I be accompanying you to your plane?"

Why else, I thought quickly. I couldn't risk admitting I didn't recognize who this man was when we met; yet for an instantaneous flash I had thought it could have been him. So quickly was my thought process when coming up with solutions: "Wait... maybe there are other possibilities here"

"I thought one of the crew would come for me," I lied.

"Oh no," Alfred explained, "they will be conducting all their safety checks at this point."

As Alfred pulled open a door for me to step through, I thanked him and found myself outside where the client's private plane gleamed brightly just metres away.

"Ms Rogers, please board whenever it suits you and I will place your luggage in the hold. Would you prefer that I keep your purse?" asked the attendant.

"Yes," I replied as I made my way toward the plane with slightly unsteady legs. As I tried to relax and let go of any thoughts of becoming the latest gold digger for someone's family, money came to mind immediately and smiles started appearing across my face - just as when it had first happened with Callie.

As I approached my plane, a flight attendant dressed in a stylish navy skirt and blazer over a white blouse warmly welcomed me by smiling wide at me.

"Hello!" I introduced myself. She welcomed me aboard and informed me that Mr Summers was waiting on the right. Please enjoy your journey."

As I approached, he stood up, his dark brown eyes blazing with evident anger as he gave a look that betrayed everything I was experiencing inside. No, it couldn't have been him; after all it wasn't. However, as soon as I entered the aisle he stood up as soon as he saw me with undisguised fury in his dark brown eyes blazing toward me with full force.

He demanded to know what was happening: 'What are you doing here AMELIA?" he inquired.

RON

RON knew this was no joke: when I told Callie I wanted a professional for this week, I meant it and had provided enough money for an expert to be hired for it.

I should have found someone more suitable. Had I desired an amateur, I could have pulled some girl from a club; however, what I required was someone who could play their role without fuss; while no sexual intimacy would take place during our act together in our shared hotel room - an arrangement in which AMELIA seemed equally happy as myself.

I looked at AMELIA, hoping she would provide an explanation, but she just stood there looking back at me silently. Nonetheless, I couldn't help noticing she was stunningly beautiful with full red lips and full cheeks that made me want to reach out and touch them. Her small nose may have been slightly off, yet this only added more vulnerability and charm than spoil her looks; moreover her long straight dark brown hair made her green eyes stand out even further.

What about her body could I say about it? Well, let's just say she had large breasts and curvier hips: an hour glass figure! Many women would kill to have her. My imagination ran wild as I imagined myself with my hands on those hips and her breasts teasing my mouth. Though casually dressed - jeans, flat black shoes and black t shirt - her beauty did not diminish at all.

Clearing my throat, I pushed away the image. No matter how good she looked, there was no way I could spend even one week with this woman; her presence had always left an unpleasant taste in my mouth, always coming across as rude or cold to people she came in contact with - almost like someone trying to be intimidating deliberately. She could easily have been someone's trophy wife; someone who took pride in being high maintenance; it wasn't something I found attractive or desirable in any way whatsoever.

"Well?" I responded when it became evident that AMELIA would not answer my query without prompting. "Why are you here?", I demanded, citing my request for an experienced counselor.

AMELIA held her head high and smiled at me, yet the smile didn't reach her eyes.

"I am a professional," she responded. "After being fired by my old boss who was an idiot and wanting me to quit quickly, it became necessary for me to find another job quickly and here we are."

"Yes, this won't work," I replied.

AMELIA approached me, appearing more confident than usual. Her face no longer exuded arrogance.

"Look, I need money," she explained, and you need someone who can act like they like you for one week - someone like herself had done just that at her workplace for years before coming over here to her job site and pretending.

"But AMELIA," I pointed out. "Do you really think I don't know you don't like me?"

"No, but you have no idea how much I dislike you and that was only me being polite to avoid openly despise." She replied.

"I don't think..." I began.
"Five minutes until take off," came a voice from behind me, as one of the cabin crew walked toward us. As she approached, AMELIA reached out and picked a piece of imaginary fluff off my shoulder in an unusually intimate gesture - prompting me to ask what she was up to until her smile lit up her whole face and made me realize just why this action had occurred.

AMELIA expressed her delight with their family by clapping her hands joyfully and exclaiming, "I can't wait to meet your family," AMELIA exclaimed, clapping enthusiastically as if in true AMELIA fashion: "especially your sister...it will be nice having one--I know I'll love her if she is anything like you."

AMELIA approached AMELIA and smiled. A cabin crew member stopped beside AMELIA and smiled warmly.

Are You Sitting Down?" she inquired.

"Certainly," AMELIA answered as she looked down at me and then looked away before looking back up again to ask: "So are you moving over or am I taking your seat on the window seat?"

"There are at least twelve other seats," I noted.

"Yes, but none are you!" she replied and smiled broadly at a cabin crew member. "Hon- estly. Who said romance is dead huh?"

"He's cute so it makes up for it," laughed one of the cabin crew members in reply.

I rolled my eyes and moved towards AMELIA who quickly sat next to me and fastened her seat belt before taking my hand in hers and absently rubbing her thumb across its backside. My skin tingled slightly wherever it touched hers - perhaps she really was professional?

"Hi, my name is Helen," explained one of the cabin crew members. "If anything arises while in flight, just let me know. Otherwise, your meal and beverage service should arrive approximately 20 minutes post take-off - is that alright?"

I nodded my head as she moved away, and pulled away my hand from AMELIA's.

"What happened?" I inquired.
She answered my query by suggesting an audition, adding, "Don't tell me it didn't work; even you were convinced when you told me there were other seats and didn't insist I leave immediately.

I sighed in disappointment as AMELIA made her case, drawing me in and convincing Helen of her act. But could she maintain it for an entire week? Ultimately I had little choice other than to let her try; AMELIA or none!

"Fine. The job is yours to do, but any misstep involving AMELIA or suspicion that all this is a scam will cost your fee dearly," he stated.

AMELIA took some time to consider this.

She spoke about their grandmother. "Your grandmother," she stated simply.

"What about her?" I replied. If your grandmother suspects this is all an elaborate hoax, my pay stops immediately," I explained. If any trusted friend doubts us and accuses us, all my pay will vanish as quickly. She explained.

"I like how you're thinking, AMELIA. Maybe this can work after all; you are on," I replied.

I held out my hand, AMELIA took it and gave a gentle shake - once more ignoring the slight tingling sensation between our palms that suggested we might soon join forces whether for good or ill. It appeared we would embark on this adventure together regardless of its outcome.

After AMELIA did her little show on the plane, she barely spoke another word to me; though this wasn't particularly bothersome to me either, but I was worried she wasn't immersing herself fully into this role. And not just on board; as soon as we landed and got off, she was all smiles and thank-yous.
Thank you to our driver for loading up her luggage into the trunk and holding open her door - yet she didn't speak a single word to me about anything!

My worries grew with each mile we traveled until finally, we reached the hotel where all the wedding events would be taking place. At that moment, I decided it was best for all parties involved to call it off, yet AMELIA had already made her escape. So instead I just got out myself, before saying another word to AMELIA or my parents showed up in front of the hotel doorway! Perfect timing.

As our driver unloaded our luggage, my parents came towards us. My mom pulled me into an embrace while I offered one back.

"Hi Mom," I asked.

"Good," she smiled warmly. "And who are these guys?"

She released me and focused her attention on AMELIA. My heart began to sink as AMELIA could potentially spoil everything if she told my mom I had paid her to be my girlfriend; or was she going to continue being moody like before?

As it turned out, AMELIA wasn't either of these things. She smiled brightly and embraced my mother warmly before air kissing each other's cheeks with air kisses that seemed as though she had done this her whole life long - maybe that had indeed been the case; I wouldn't know.

AMELIA welcomed Mrs Summers enthusiastically: "I'm AMELIA; RON told me about you."

"Well then," my mom responded in frustration. She swiped my arm as she spoke: "Raf here has kept himself all to himself; he has been extremely mysterious about who exactly you are; in fact he wouldn't even tell me your name when asked; all he would say was that he wanted me to meet someone new.

AMELIA smiled back. "Well, that much I hope," she gestured down at herself and added: "Don't think for one second that this outfit was suitable to meet you; I thought we would have plenty of time to get to our rooms and change first."

"Don't you look lovely? Doesn't she look lovely Harry?" my mom exclaimed in surprise.

My dad, used to my mother's energetic exuberance and content to remain silent most of the time, simply nodded his head and smiled reassuringly.

"Yes," AMELIA replied. "Nice to meet you." Summers smiled and then introduced himself as her partner in crime.

"Let's stop with all this "Mr & Mrs Summers nonsense", my mom warned AMELIA as she tied AMELIA's arm into Harry's. My mom then led AMELIA inside. Sofia introduced herself as Harry then said they should grab a drink together while meeting other members and collecting luggage/checking in. Harry took over to collect their luggage/check-in their room if required by my mother.

"No," AMELIA replied quickly.

My mom quickly replied with, "Don't take offense," in order to put us all at ease. We only planned on having one quick drink at the bar.

AMELIA graciously gave in and allowed my mom to lead her away, with me following close behind as they chatted away and asked AMELIA questions which she answered fully and with interest. After seeing how adept AMELIA was at manipulating my feelings when we were alone, I could accept if she turned off her charm when we were alone - now that I had seen how easy she could switch it on or off like a tap, this would actually be welcomed by me!

Once we reached the bar, my mom, AMELIA, and I entered at once. There were only a few tables occupied at first but eventually I spotted my family sitting at one table: grandma Sammy was sitting alongside my sister and Eve my niece - instantly recognisable by me!
Sammy was engaged to Bradley and I noticed his side of the family wasn't there at all - perhaps there was some sort of bride drama thing? To be honest, I didn't really care either way as weddings used to last just one day back then! Now weddings last weeks long with endless tasks I would rather

avoid doing altogether; weddings weren't really my cup of tea anyway so don't hold it against me if this seems odd to you.

My irritable feeling subsided significantly when my grandmother rose from her chair and came towards me. She pinched my cheeks which could have been embarrassing; had it been anyone else, it would likely have been worse; yet whenever my grandmother did something to me I found it tolerable and found her actions comforting instead of embarrassing.

"Darling boy," she smiled and pulled me in for a hug, "it has been too long. One of these times you will leave me abandoned and when you come back and visit me later on, you may even find me dead!"

"Don't get all melodramatic," I replied with laughter. "We only saw each other last Tuesday - not even two weeks!"

"Yes," my grandmother acknowledged, "but you should have seen the look on that poppet's face when I started speaking.

My grandmother then gestured towards AMELIA, who came forward and smiled sweetly at my grandparent before turning away to hug my chest.

"I'm delighted to meet you," AMELIA exclaimed.

My grandmother replied with a wink: "Don't be so sure." You might just find out I'm quite cranky now!

My dad joked, joining us around the table. "Well, that you are mother," he noted. "But we still love you."

My grandmother made a fistshake gesture towards my dad before laughingly hugging AMELIA. While they were hugging, my father gave me our room key card - room 519. I glanced over it.

My grandma welcomed AMELIA warmly into our family, saying: 'Welcome. You seem like one who may stay."

As soon as she said it, I felt simultaneously guilty and relieved at how well my plan had worked. My grandmother was in her early nineties and seemed as healthy as ever - I knew this could change quickly with age though so wanted her to think I had found someone. She had long dreamt of seeing me settle down with someone, so it would give her great satisfaction to think this happened for real!

"That is the plan," AMELIA replied with a smile to my grandmother. I then introduced AMELIA as being my grandmother's granddaughter:

As I introduced AMELIA and Sammy, both smiled back. After my grandma returned to her seat, I introduced

AMELIA and Eve again; both smiled back as AMELIA scooped Eve up immediately onto her hip with cooing praises for how adorable Eve was. Eve surprised everyone again by reaching up her arms for AMELIA to pick her up; AMELIA swiftly did just that and began cooing over how adorable Eve was.

Sammy couldn't believe what was happening: Bradley usually only wanted her close, such as with us or his parents; she wasn't even drawn towards my best friend who is her godmother! " I can't believe this," Sammy exclaimed in shock, shaking her head in disbelief. "She usually seems quite attached."

My mom smiled at AMELIA as she pulled out a chair for her to sit down. "You must be quite good," my mother exclaimed with admiration.

AMELIA sat down and thanked Eve, placing her onto AMELIA's lap.

Sammy asked AMELIA if she had children of her own. "AMELIA, do you have children of your own?" Sammy inquired.

AMELIA replied in the negative. To her own admission, AMELIA never wanted children and cringed as my family all fell silent before Sammy broke it all off with one words of his own:

"Raf and you may not make the ideal pair, then. He wants at least four children," she noted.

Before I could respond, AMELIA burst out laughing and nodded in agreement.

"He made it abundantly clear it was an issue for him, and I have come around to the idea. Prior to meeting RON, I always assumed I wouldn't want children due to not finding someone I could see as being their father. Now I believe otherwise!"

She turned around and smiled, then squeezed my hand, making an exasperated scene more tolerable almost effortlessly. Callie could only do this so well! But this woman really had some serious skills when it came to defusing situations.

My dad went up to the bar and returned shortly with an ice bucket and bottle of champagne; shortly thereafter a bartender followed with a tray full of champagne flutes for us all to use; they all took one glass each while our bartender poured our drinks for us, before toasting Sammy and Bradley and their new life together.

Conversation flowed quickly as drinks were served and soon, Bradley, his parents, Melissa (Sammy's best friend and her maid of honor), Liam (Bradley's best man) and Bradley joined us - but other bridesmaids/groomsmen hadn't arrived yet and I found myself quietly wondering how they managed to avoid me?

My mom realized how late it had become only when she announced she was hungry and I saw it was already past nine o'clock. We decided that no one really wanted to change, so rather than go through to the restaurant we ordered bar meals and stayed right where we were before finishing up eating our meals and heading back out again. Soon afterwards we were back home.
At some point, Sammy excused herself so Eve could come upstairs to bed.

As evening turned to night, the lights dimmed down in the bar and a disco began. I knew I must have been drunk when AMELIA grabbed my hand and pulled me to my feet.

"Let's Dance," AMELIA suggested. I wasn't initially persuaded, but somehow found myself following her to the half full dance floor and soon enough we were laughing and dancing, twirling each other around, and laughing at our own performances (or perhaps only mine); whatever, it didn't matter because I was having so much fun; maybe AMELIA was playing her part all too well - whatever; whatever!

Whatever! Whatever, it didn't matter as long as everyone could enjoy themselves tonight - everyone kept reminding me that weddings were meant to be enjoyable events!

By the time the disco ended and lights came back up in the bar, I was both happily tired and somewhat breathless. AMELIA and I returned to our table where we said our farewells to those still finishing off their drinks before leaving and heading for the elevator.

"We're in room five nineteen," I announced, and AMELIA hit the button for the fifth floor. She noted: "I think my family might like you better than they like me."

"Who could blame them?" AMELIA asked with a laugh, smiling as she added that her popularity among her peers was due to being naturally likeable.

"And are you saying I am wrong?" I joked to her.

"You seem to do an exceptional job of concealing your nicer qualities than I do. Can I ask why?" she inquired.

"Not perfect but I'll take it," I replied with a smile.

As soon as the elevator reached our floor, we started walking down the hallway counting off other rooms until we reached our own. About halfway down I used my key card to open our room door by pushing it open wider - then counted off all other rooms as we went along the corridor.

AMELIA seemed relieved to follow my request and entered the room, smiling thank-you and entering first.

"Nice," she exclaimed as she took in her surroundings.

In the middle of a decent-sized room was a four poster bed with small bedside cabinets either side. Opposite the bed was a desk with chair, featuring an enormous flat screen television. A full length couch in one corner seemed comfortable enough for sleeping; and there was also a wardrobe and chest of drawers along the opposite wall from where the door stood - not bad at all!

AMELIA began making her way through the room as I inserted my key card into the slot for electric, turning on all of its lights. Once inside I closed and locked the door before watching as AMELIA opened up the bathroom door to peek inside; over her shoulder I could see into its interior; it wasn't huge, but more than adequate with its decent-sized shower, separate bath tub, double sink beneath mirror with plenty of toiletries to choose from for our use.

At first glance, it wasn't exactly my dream wedding venue, but it certainly served its purpose well and as long as Sammy was happy, who am I to complain?

AMELIA emerged from the bathroom and opened her suitcase, pulling out an elegant red silk night gown that she smiled and pointed at me for me to see.

"I won't take too long," she announced before entering the bathroom.

Before I could settle onto the couch, I needed to wait for AMELIA's return from using the toilet and brushing my teeth; while waiting I began unpacking my suitcase while doing so. Soon enough she emerged out of the bathroom; taking my breath away by having removed all her make up in an amazing display that left me speechless.
As she brushed her hair out, I noticed she looked equally stunning with and without makeup and hair styling.

Amazing night dress. She looked incredible. The material was thin and shiny red; the straps were thin spaghetti straps; its neckline edged in black lace for an eye-catching finish; it fit just perfectly on her hips while showing off her curves perfectly; my only question was why her nipples poked out of its thin material so hard; it wasn't cold in the room.

"Wow," I exclaimed, unable to contain my excitement at her sight.

AMELIA smiled softly as her cheeks turned pink at my praise, turning down slightly to peer up at me through her long dark eyelashes.

"Do you like it?" She asked me in one way of putting it. Without trusting myself to articulate, I nodded and nodded again before standing up to go into the bathroom myself and finding AMELIA standing there; as soon as she left I stood up and cleared my throat before heading towards it myself and found myself face-to-face with AMELIA who started moving her right leg slightly before I did so as well, with neither one moving in any particular direction; then in response we both went together, yet suddenly being so close was no longer awkward nor was my body reacting funny at being so close; instead there was nothing funny about me reacting negatively towards her presence - my body just felt strange about responding so quickly to seeing her!

Before I could rationalize it away, I reached out and clasped AMELIA's head between my two hands and pulled her closer, pressing my lips against hers as I pulled. AMELIA began moaning into my mouth as her body pressed against mine; I could feel the cool silk of her night dress as well as heat coming through my clothes from her skin; my hand worked its way into her hair while another rested briefly on her ass before moving it towards front of AMELIA's body.
I slid my hand up her inner thigh, beneath the silky material of her night dress and discovered AMELIA's already wet slit.

Pushing my fingers between her lips, I found AMELIA's pulsing clit and began massaging it back and forth between side to side to make AMELIA cry out as I massaged it back and forth between front to back while deepening our kiss by interlocking tongues between us.

I wanted to taste, touch, and fuck her. I needed that hot, wet little pussy tight around my hard cock. So, I pulled my mouth from hers and kissed down her neck and across her shoulder before pulling up on AMELIA's night gown hem and tugging up. AMELIA took my hint and took off her gown over her head before dropping it alongside us on the ground beside us. As I worked her clit, I kissed down her chest then took one of AMELIA's nipples into my own mouth before pulling myself off from hers and kissing down her chest before sucking one into my own mouth - so much pleasure was had that night gown?

As I worked her, she reached towards me and opened my belt; then pushed her hand inside my boxer shorts before wrapping her fist around my cock - her movements mimicking those I was using on her - taking my breath away before I had to release her breast to catch my breath before becoming overcome by exhaustion.

No matter. She was so close to climax that one more hard press on her clit was enough to push her over the edge. For an instant, her hand stopped moving up and down on me instead gripping my cock tightly as her head went back and the tendons on her neck stood out; as soon as that happened she let out a moan before lifting back up her head again and looking at me with surprise.

Her pupils dilated with desire at my gaze, her lips pink from our passionate kissing, her chest moving as she gasped for breath as I knew that, without my intervention, she'd soon work me again as she put in another turn in me and continued working me until finally I pulled away and let her do it all on me again.
Soon enough, she would rip her hand away and this would all be over before we had even begun.

I grabbed AMELIA's wrist and pulled her hand free from my boxer shorts, kissed her again, and began walking her towards the bed shedding my clothes along the way. We reached it, whereupon I pushed AMELIA onto it from behind until she fell on top of me perfectly positioned on its surface - exactly where I wanted her.

As soon as AMELIA had made room, I quickly removed my socks and shoes - the only items still left on me. Climbing onto the bed, she quickly scooted backwards to make room for me. Opening her legs wide to show moisture on her slit and pussy opening, I could feel AMELIA inviting me inside her. Kneeling between her legs I slowly lowered myself on top of her, aligning my cock with her pussy, releasing my long stroke inside AMELIA before entering AMELIA completely, making AMELIA full.

She gasped as I collided into her, her hands coming up to wrap around my shoulders. Slowly at first, I began thrusting inside of her, enjoying the warm tightness against me as we kissed as I moved further inside of her and her hands roamed freely across my back, sides, ass, cheeks until they finally went all the way in until my talons had fully penetrated her body.

She allowed me to move for another second before she bucked her hips unexpectedly and I found myself completely surprised, rolling to one side while we both rolled towards AMELIA who then came on top of me to join in her moves as her breasts bounced wildly up and down in time with each thrust. It was an impressive sight.

Her skin was covered in a thin sheen of sweat that shimmered like she was almost iridescent against the moonlight that still trickled through through open curtains. As she worked us both up into an uproarious frenzy, her long locks whipped around her face as she worked us both into an even greater frenzy - pushing one hand down her flat stomach while also pressing her fingers between lips as she rode me.
As I watched AMELIA perform her show, my breath caught in my throat; she was incredible hot. After waiting patiently until AMELIA reached climax, it was time for me to buck my hips and throw AMELIA off balance. Once back on top of

her I began increasing the frequency and pace of my thrusts so she had no respite; panting and gasping for breath as warm liquid began oozing from her, pressing against my shoulder pressed against it while also digging her nails into my back - fearful that she might float away if she let go.

As her orgasm surged through her body, her pussy clenched more tightly around me - it sealed the deal for me! Heat was radiating off of both cock and stomach before I felt pleasure tingle throughout my body like nothing ever had before - taking me places I never knew existed!

My cock gave one last spasm, and the pleasure was more intense than anything I'd experienced. AMELIA and I laid in bed side-by-side gasping for air, both stunned that this woman, by far the most annoying I had ever met, turned out to be by far my greatest source of sex pleasure ever experienced - there had to be some kind of irony somewhere here; surely some sort of surprise factor had taken place?

As soon as we had finally recovered, I got up and went to use the bathroom, just like I had intended to earlier.

As soon as I finished what was necessary, I returned into the main room where AMELIA lay sleeping peacefully on her back with her head turned towards me and one hand resting against a pillow beside her face. Her eyes were closed while lips slightly parted while goose bumps covered her skin - and I could feel something cool in the air now too.

As I didn't want AMELIA to freeze during the night, I carefully moved her duvet from beneath her and placed it over her shoulders.
At first she made no sense; then I couldn't understand anything she said; finally she gave a soft snore, followed by even breathing again and I smiled down at her. Although my original plan had been for us to sleep together in bed after we had had sex, now that AMELIA had fallen asleep while I was gone it felt somehow inappropriate so instead, reluctantly, I went into my wardrobe to retrieve an extra pillow and blanket before lying down on the sofa instead.

AMELIA

I woke slowly, straining to break free from an otherwise restful and refreshing sleep. Rubbing my hand across my eyes, I yawned as memories came rushing back into my mind and my brain took over to sort them all out.

Recalling having sex with RON had been the last thing on my agenda; yet in that moment it felt right. RON had been nothing but attentive all night long; although I knew he was acting, there was something alluring about him that made me attracted to him; when he kissed me it just felt right!

He wasn't in my bed next to me and when I looked around for him to appear I expected to see him getting dressed or using the bathroom, but no such luck; instead he was sound asleep on the couch having spent most of the night there after having left our bed when we both fell asleep.

I wasn't entirely sure of my feelings towards any of this, but RON being on the couch told me exactly how he felt: regretful that we made such a mess of our relationship, yet agreeable enough to admit we made mistakes and move on together. We could put all this behind us quickly enough and move on together as friends.
Decision made, I quietly got out of bed while remaining mindful that RON could suddenly wake up any minute and see me without clothes on. Perhaps my response had been

unreasonable but now that he had chosen not to share my bed I couldn't help feeling this way.

After entering the bathroom and procuring a fluffy white towel to wrap myself with, I made my way back into my bedroom where I went through my suitcase to select white three quarter length pants and yellow vest top for that day as well as underwear and my toiletries bag before heading into the bathroom again.

After taking a shower and washing my hair, brushing my teeth, drying off, getting dressed and gathering up my dirty laundry from last night I headed back into my bedroom.

RON spoke first. Whilst still sitting on the couch, but now sitting up, with blanket folded neatly in front of him. Wearing nothing other than white boxer shorts he reminded me instantly of how his skin had felt against mine, how hard his movements had made me come and almost had me fainting with pleasure. I could smell his scent now…

"Good morning!" I said with as much ease as possible.

RON had lost my resolve, as seeing his naked, muscular chest had shaken my resolve. So I began unpacking my clothes to hang them up alongside his, more so as a way of turning my back to him without being rude than any real desire to stop living out of my suitcase.

RON spoke up from behind me as I began placing my underwear into one of the drawers.

"So about last night," he began. It sounded as if he didn't quite know what to say next, but since he hadn't brought up this subject myself I wasn't about to provide him a quick solution; instead I made a hmm sound and waited.
"I... well, I wanted to apologize. I don't know what came over me - maybe it was all the drinking and dancing and that night dress you wore... Yeah. Maybe it shouldn't have come out this way."

I shrugged my shoulders and eventually turned towards him.

"It wasn't entirely one-sided; we both consumed too much alcohol and things happened as they should," I stated with a grin.

RON agreed. "So what now?" he continued, "can't we just pretend nothing happened and move forward with our week-long activities?"

"Yes," I responded. "Let's keep things professional going forward." RON nodded and seemed ready to say something but then looked away before turning around again.

He gave his head a slight shake and when he spoke again it didn't correspond with my expectations: "I need to quickly shower and dress before we head out for breakfast; I'm starving."

My stomach decided it was time for an eruption, and we all laughed it off together.

"That should do," I responded as RON made his way towards the bathroom, while I sat down at my desk to put on makeup. This hadn't gone half as badly as expected!

"OH WOW THAT'S AMAZING," I exclaimed as I took a bite of bacon sandwich.

Bread was fresh and soft; bacon was deliciously crispy and salty; Evelyn looked up from her tea cup, smiled warmly at me while sipping, then laughed softly as we laughed together over our treat!

"That reminds me of something from when RON was still young," she replied.

RON protested, but we all knew she would tell the tale regardless and we all laughed knowingly at his indulgent laughter, knowing full well she would tell it anyway. "No Grandma!" RON ordered, but we all knew he wouldn't stop her any further than already had done.

"RON always loved bacon when he was small, often eating it for breakfast, lunch and dinner if allowed by his parents," Evelyn reminisced. "One day we took him and Sammy on an excursion to a working farm where animals could be petted and fed while looking around all of the equipment available there - Raf fell in love with a little piglet named Shirley whom he eventually had to leave behind; although when it came time to leave him behind again he eventually got over his sadness; however as far as we knew, that was that."

"But that wasn't all. A few months after Shirley had all but been forgotten about, RON came home from daycare crying inconsolably and refused to tell anyone why. His mom eventually got him talking about bacon being made from pork pigs - something which reminded him of Shirley and how one day someone would consume her flesh. That day RON decided he no longer liked bacon - this decision lasted two or three years before he wanted any again! My husband was still alive then; when asked by RON what changed his mind he replied that one day with an answer like: Shirley will long been consumed before I care for the other pigs."

RON and I laughed along with her. She was truly entertaining, her story even more so, knowing when and how long to pause before carrying on. When she saw us laughing she smiled warmly; so I took full advantage of this situation while still maintaining my role of being the good girlfriend.

"Any more embarrassing stories about RON?" I inquired, hoping for any further stories about him. When Evelyn responded with "There was the time when he got completely obsessed with his little willy," Evelyn gave a laugh before giving us more details of their exploits as RON became completely obsessed with their willy.

"No, Grandma," RON answered.

"Please hush now," Evelyn told me with an eye toward me. She glanced over and pointed towards Evelyn before asking, "You want to hear this right?"

"Certainly," I replied. RON stood up, and at first I thought he was leaving angrily; then, as he moved toward the doorway he smiled knowingly before shaking his head with satisfaction and turning around to face me and shake hands before leaving again.

"I can't talk you out of it, so let me get you some tea Grandma," he suggested.

As RON left, Evelyn smiled warmly at me.

"He wasn't even three when it all began, yet somehow discovered his willy one morning," Evelyn recounted, as we laughed out loud at Evelyn's comment about Harry constantly touching it through his clothes, according to Evelyn's account. When this problem continued at day care as well as home, Sofia and Harry got called into a meeting with the centre manager and went in together wondering why their attendance was necessary for any such meeting." When this occurred in day care it became even worse: two parents were called together in for such meetings before meeting ended in confusion; eventually both parents left feeling overwhelmed by its severity." Evelyn concluded by saying it would only get worse; Harry would find himself attending these meetings wondering what would be so important they both would needing to attend them."

"They arrived and the manager informed them that RON had developed the habit of pulling down his pants and underwear and holding onto his willy without actually playing with it," Evelyn explained.

"Oh no!" I shrieked with laughter, unable to stop myself from picturing it all in my mind. Tears streamed down my face as Evelyn nodded her head.

"That was Harry and Sofia's response; however, Evelyn reported that the day care centre manager did not find this at all amusing and informed them that RON no longer belonged there," Evelyn reported.

"Grandma likes to brag that I got kicked out of a day care center for touching my willy," RON continued, as he returned with another pot of tea for Evelyn. He could only imagine the stunned silence that followed such an announcement.

At first I laughed so hard I was on the verge of snorting, but eventually managed to contain myself slightly. Evelyn nodded her approval at RON's statement.

Evelyn said it was great fun doing that and gave an explanation. After her explanation was complete, her colleagues concluded it must have been because of Evelyn being old so they didn't understand properly, rather I let them believe they had the answer when in reality we knew differently; RON?

RON made a grunting sound which could have meant anything; Evelyn seemed content enough to interpret it as agreement. RON quickly made her another cup of tea with milk as promised.

"Please use caution," he warned her when she reached for it, as the meat could still be hot from its fresh state.

Evelyn stroked my lower arm before smiling at me and then him.

She smiled sweetly. "You must already know this," she replied, "but just in case..."

I smiled and nodded my head; there wasn't much else I could do as part of my role.

RON abruptly told her to stop speaking about herself so loudly; yet I could see that he was trying hard not to smile in response to her praise.

He really seemed to adore Evelyn, and being around her brought out an entirely different side of him - gentleness and caring were hallmarks of affection in him that I hadn't noticed previously. With each interaction between them I saw more evidence of his sweet side; maybe his cold hard exterior wasn't all there after all?
Maybe outside of work he was just genuinely kind-hearted person.

Stop it, I told myself. Don't even begin going there.

Making out with RON was easy - there was no disputing his attractiveness - but she couldn't stand him as an individual.

RON

As I waited for AMELIA, I stared out the restaurant window. It appeared to be a pleasant day outside, so perhaps AMELIA and I should make plans together?

At lunch, I suggested going for a stroll around the grounds afterward. Although she'd been friendly towards me, sometimes it could be hard to keep track of reality versus fiction; therefore I thought spending some time alone would clear away any blurred lines and remind me what it was I really disliked about her; or perhaps actively disliked might be more appropriate?

Though I dislike AMELIA, I still enjoyed having sex with her the other night. Was that weird? Possibly; however, two consenting adults met and decided they wanted sex together; regardless of our opinion about each other or dislike for AMELIA personally, no denying she is hot; in any event it wouldn't have been human of me not wanting sex with her!

On the morning after, I pretended to regret what had occurred as AMELIA seemed upset; thinking it would make things simpler if I said I regretted my action as well, we could proceed as planned and business would remain normal between us.
Now onward, speaking my truth would have been better: no regrets and openness towards repeating it again.

Before I saw her wearing that nightdress, I never imagined myself having sexual relations with her. Sure, she was physically attractive; however, that didn't excuse the way she always treated me coldly and spoke of me with derision in her voice - making me question how any one could like her when not performing an act.

But even now she was acting disrespectfully towards me, even while being paid to do otherwise. After making some work-related calls this morning, I had arranged to meet AMELIA for lunch here at the restaurant and she should have arrived five minutes ago - even if there had been genuine reasons, wouldn't being polite and notifying me would have sufficed?

As time passed and I felt myself growing increasingly annoyed, I checked my watch again and saw that ten minutes had already gone by since our scheduled meeting time. Decidently I got up and left the restaurant in search of the elevators so when AMELIA finally came into town she wouldn't find me sitting around like some kind of idiot waiting for her.

As I stormed down the hallway, I heard AMELIA's voice calling my name. To my displeasure, however, she wasn't anywhere to be found - which meant she must be somewhere within earshot yet I couldn't see her at this particular spot -

suggesting she must be somewhere inside one of the bars - which made my irritation escalate even further since this meant she was more likely drinking than meeting me! Great.

I knew a public argument would not be in our best interests. But I couldn't allow AMELIA to take advantage of my facade without speaking up, which was unacceptable and unconstitutional. So as I approached the bar I realized AMELIA wasn't actually drinking; she was sitting with Sammy with Eve's sippy cup sitting empty on their table in front of them. So as soon as I reached its door I did just that. I went in, approached AMELIA but saw she wasn't actually consuming any alcohol; in fact she wasn't even really in there at all; instead she was sitting together with Sammy rather than actually engaging me; this time though it seemed more appropriate! So I went in through and found AMELIA sitting together with Sammy with Eve sitting beside them with Eve sippy cup holding Eve on Eves sippy cup sitting on their table instead - something neither of us were doing at all. Upon reaching AMELIA sitting by Sammy at doorway I saw she wasn't actually drinking herself; instead sitting with Sammy and wasn't actually in fact drinking anything; instead she was sitting together sitting with Sammy while not drinking alcohol herself either; instead I saw she wasn't actually doing much more. On arriving I realized AMELIA wasn't drinking at all despite appearances supposed drink in front of them at all seated next to Eves sippy cup sitting before them all in front of course.. if only that time would'd's sippy cup would's ia would's.

Sammy was crying while AMELIA held an arm around her while speaking. I knew I should move away but decided not to because it intrigued me more. Soon enough I understood what was going on: Sammy was having doubts about marrying Bradley, which caused AMELIA to calm her down by helping her see why it would still make sense to marry Bradley as she loved Bradley enough and that it would still make an excellent life partner despite any freak-outs closer to the wedding date. At the same time she kept Eve entertained by drawing shadow characters on walls that kept making shadows ducks rabbits and more characters on walls which kept Eve amused while keeping Eve amused at once more.

Eve sat contentedly on AMELIA's lap, laughing happily at shadow creatures. Seeing AMELIA comfort my sister while entertaining Eve slightly softened my feelings; though Sammy being in tears may have been more important than lunch arrangements; still, I was disappointed she hadn't bothered to notify me first.

I decided to still go up to my room, and when AMELIA texted to see where I was when she arrived at the restaurant to find me, I would come down again and forgive her for being late while making sure we communicate about anything that came up later.

As I made my way towards the elevator, my cell phone began ringing with more work calls I'd need to make. Although I would have rather turned it off completely, the world didn't stop turning due to a wedding and consequently neither could my business. With an excellent manager already in place who handled things seamlessly throughout the day.
My life was mostly uneventful and most other tasks went smoothly too; no complaints there!

My heart sank as I realized the ping sound hadn't signaled a voicemail from a client or manager; rather, my cell phone displayed a text message from AMELIA instead. As soon as I opened and read it, it was short and sweet - everything I expected.

"I apologize. Unfortunately, I am running late. Please feel free to eat without me and if necessary I can grab something later if necessary x"

As I read her message and saw its time stamp, it dawned on me: AMELIA had sent the text twenty minutes prior to our meeting time - she had not only comforted my sister while taking care of my niece but had also done exactly the right thing - my lack of signal had been more of an issue than her lack of manners.

Feeling embarrassed, I turned around and headed back into the restaurant. After sitting at my original table again, an anxious looking AMELIA burst through and saw me. Immediately she headed towards our table to join us before quickly sitting herself down next to me at my table.

"I'm sorry," she apologized, before responding "It's OK". Continuing, I asked what had transpired to make her late for work: What happened and why are you here now?"

Of course I knew the answers, but in AMELIA's mind I hadn't known where she had been and it would look odd not asking.

AMELIA explained, "I was simply helping Sammy with wedding stuff that will likely bore you. However, time just flew by."

I smiled and nodded silently to AMELIA as I silently awarded her another points for not gossiping and protecting Sammy during his moment of vulnerability.

AMELIA asked, grasping a menu in her hands: "Should we order something?".
I nodded and took up my menu too. Earlier, I'd wondered why people liked AMELIA so much; now I was starting to understand why: when she wasn't around me, her cold

exterior melted away, opening up just slightly more; people may like this version of her -- I certainly would have.

We ordered lunch - I ordered tuna salad while she went for the jacket potato with cheese - and chatted while waiting.

"Sammy mentioned taking some time off work and traveling through Europe last night," AMELIA observed. "Did you do that too?"

"No," I replied. "Sammy works as a graphic designer, meaning she can work from pretty much anywhere with an internet connection, including during her year's travels. By contrast, my business selling sportswear wholesale doesn't allow for as much travel; therefore I decided not to participate."

"Wouldn't your parents consider hiring an interim manager or something similar if they wanted out before you were quite prepared to take over?" she inquired.

"My business wasn't run by my parents," I replied to her, "but by myself.

"Oh, sorry!" AMELIA replied. "I always assumed you inherited your father's business."

I shook my head again, ready to talk about the line of work of my father when the waiter brought our food. We both

thanked him, then began feasting upon our meal. Throughout our conversation we didn't focus on one specific topic but rather just chatted generally - AMELIA told me about her trip to Thailand for six weeks over her summer holidays before starting college - showing me some sights she saw there and telling me about its history and culture. She shared some details with me of her trip that surprised me immensely!
She vividly remembered the places she had visited and passionately recounted them to us.

I was struck by her infectious enthusiasm, and for an instant could hardly remember why AMELIA had always seemed cold to me.

AMELIA

On the night before my wedding, we attended the rehearsal dinner - an elaborate affair featuring seven courses which left me completely full to capacity - which wasn't ideal.

RON and I remained the only members from our party still in the bar after everyone had started leaving; all the rest had left because no one wanted to get sick while attending a wedding ceremony. But since no one wanted to risk leaving too early, RON and I had decided to remain. Now it was just us two at this particular establishment!

On our second night here it was much calmer - there was no disco to keep people entertained; just some gentle music played softly in the background, and we actually managed to hold an actual conversation without degenerating into bickering and then argument between RON and myself - something which normally would happen within moments. But tonight was different - we talked like civilized adults who might actually like each other!

At first, when RON spoke, I wasn't trying to act the part of an engaged girlfriend; I just was myself and found myself listening carefully when he spoke. His attentiveness when listening was reciprocated when speaking, so it didn't feel forced at all. When speaking my turn, RON seemed just as attentive; this didn't feel forced either.

No one else was around, and while I took his lead and followed his instruction for performing my act, he paid for my service. If he wanted, he could just tell me to stop performing and go away; no one needed this activity anyway - but instead he didn't.

"What will happen when your father retires?" I inquired after RON mentioned how many hours were being put into running his business.

What will happen if I send him home?", asked another student. "Nothing bad will happen! He will remain home."

RON suggested taking his mother on a cruise.

If he had been behaving as I expected him to, I may have mistaken him for being deliberately provocative, but instead felt that he missed the point of my questions altogether.

"I meant with his business," I clarified, "will you manage it alongside your own, or will Sammy run it as part of hers, or will he just sell it off?"

"My father doesn't own any businesses," he responded to my inquiry about him being a billion-aire bachelor, as though my wealth came solely from my parents' assets. At that moment he smiled broadly at my confusion before explaining that one of those annoying articles about his success made assumptions that I obtained my wealth through their parents rather than working hard myself.

My line of questioning had made it obvious what my response would be; therefore, there was no point in trying to deny what had already become apparent to everyone in the room. I nodded my head. There was no sense in denying my thoughts now.

"To start off, I am not quite a billionaire - though certainly multi-millionaires", RON explained. "That said, my money could have made me one if I'd been more greedy with it; however, that is not my style; my business is completely my own and was started when I left college - perhaps you could say I "fell lucky", though this would not be accurate - all earnings come directly from me alone." RON noted: "My father never owned his own business either; instead he worked as mechanic for garage near where we lived when growing up while my mom worked as cashier in 7-11s around town while being raised. Both parents worked full time jobs in garages or seven elevens nearby while being raised. So neither possessed any formal knowledge or skills as they didn't own business of their own; both worked as mechanics at garages close by when growing up whereas neither had business interests of their own; however they did however provide income." RON explained. "Neither parent had business experience either; neither did my father; however; however; however both worked at garage nearby when growing up while mom worked as cashier at 7-11s that were close by. Both worked there were employed with 7-11s while both worked there to provide income," RON continued "My mother worked at 711's, all through schooling; as cashiers themselves until becoming successful," RON noted." RON continued. "Somehow just got lucky enough!" RON explained. My Father never started his own right before they took place; only then saw opportunity. Although my parents never owned businesses themselves before started off when she worked her own; both worked elsewhere before she worked 'cathen worked their own 711s that was employed near where she worked at seven.. My Dad worked nearby garage mechanic jobs too while working down the same area they did work too and only cashiers while working alongside my parents worked primarily until she worked there was used. Both worked also. My Dad worked while also worked cashiers for 711s was there. Somewhere some were also worked when young but she would only ever so so "something ac." My Dad wasn't either way; neither ran her mother too "Someone who were only ever ran either one other than either when she did before she worked. Somehow". While my mother worked while working while so did some when we lived.. but worked cashiers during those near where they did; some worked just down the Road near our lived while my mom. some never ran 7 11s. Some other used either at other garage down just across town where she did when we lived (s!! (only." had had neither was actually used too until soon after having just...some when she worked"....some too!" RON spoke before. Somehow did her as she worked untill's only ever before them later than them worked them anyway). Some were working too." Some... They also made out." Although his did too..." (because both father didn's too... ".) Some used my dad; when growing up until one!) whils!), while worked until just...and me as she did!) either!" (though), and only working....) for them too...!) while also work before; just so!!! before!" Headed them! =). She made.." worked by themselves!" RON." Of course. Since his) did' as cashiers with someone else would'd until too!"!). Sometimes where?) just where but they gave some sorting him.... Some may Have'n". Whiles too!!" Some. They might have but Sammy and I never went without money though; every month there was enough to cover expenses.

"I am shocked," I stated, "as I always assumed..."

I paused, uncertain of how to end this sentence. RON smiled warmly.

"You assumed I was some spoiled brat who'd grown up with everything handed to him and just been given Daddy's company to play at running while the board took on all of the hard work," he stated. "Right?"

"Almost," I answered honestly, "but I never imagined you weren't working hard; rather, I always assumed you were making some sort of statement about him or something else.

RON laughed and shrugged.

"No. As previously stated, growing up there wasn't always enough money. When I became an adult and looked back on my childhood years, this became apparent: My parents never let Sammy or me know they were struggling financially - they went without things but not us - so from the moment it hit home I made a commitment that there would never again be weeks without enough funds," he explained. After working for several years he paid off their mortgage as well as providing other items they might otherwise decline receiving from him (this latter move sometimes leaves them no choice than accepting what comes their way from me despite their resistance!). After working for several years he managed to pay off their mortgage as well as make other contributions - which left them no choice but accept.

"Your parents must feel lucky to have you as their teacher," I replied.

RON replied. After draining his glass and standing up, he asked, "Same again?" "Yes."

I nodded as RON made his way towards the bar. Now I understood just how misinformed my impression had been; this wasn't some rich child; this wasn't some man with money who wanted to show how much he appreciated his family and showed it with gifts and cards.

He was actually quite sweet. Once I realized this and didn't immediately discredit his words, I knew I was in trouble.

RON

AMELIA took an unexpectedly keen interest in me. She seemed truly shocked that my hard work had allowed me to obtain what I have accomplished.

AMELIA seemed touched to hear how I took care of both my parents and grandmother. In addition, I gave generously to charity without wanting AMELIA to feel that I was bragging or making myself out as better than she really was.

AMELIA wasn't necessary putting on her act since there were only me and she from our group present, unlike when it had happened elsewhere in which she didn't bother. So it meant I had to believe, no matter how unlikely it seemed, that AMELIA wasn't all bad; when her guard down she could actually be quite nice. This brought back memories of how cold she seemed toward me before realizing why; thus prompting me to inquire with AMELIA why that had always been so. While things seemed good between us both, I decided I was going to ask AMELIA why that had always seemed cold to me before realising what it had become known - while things went well, I planned on asking AMELIA about why.
As soon as I arrived at the table with our drinks, I sat down. AMELIA thanked me and I held up my glass in gratitude.

"To old enemies becoming new friends," I replied, hoping I hadn't misread the situation and made myself look foolish with such an inappropriate toast. If this had been the case, my awkward words may have come off sounding rather foolish indeed.

AMELIA smiled as she clinked her glass against mine and laughed out loud.

"Here's to old enemies becoming new friends!" she repeated with a smile before sipping from her glass and taking another sip from it.

"So far tonight you've asked me many questions about myself and my life. Let me pose one for you to consider," I suggested.

AMELIA signalled for me to continue.

"When I met you for the first time, I assumed you were one of those trophy wife women - attractive but miserable, like smiling would make your face crack; someone wealthy would come along, marry you both and then you would all live unhappily ever after," I stated.

"Oh no," AMELIA responded with laughter, "that couldn't be further from the truth! I would much prefer being single than being in an unhappy relationship."

"Well, I have come to think that my impression of you might have been inaccurate. Over the last week I have witnessed your mask slip a few times and you aren't as much of an ice queen as you make out to be. So here's my question for you; why are you so cold and distant with me? And please don't say it's because you don't like me because this behavior started before we had enough of an opportunity for that exchange," I posed my query.

"I wouldn't call me cold to you," AMELIA replied, yet kept her gaze away from mine when making this comment.

"Right," I replied. "And so the chill blains I used to get whenever you looked at me in the office weren't due to you?"

AMELIA let out a short, indignant laugh before shaking her head and looking directly at me when speaking again.
"It's nothing personal," she responded, "it's just that I keep at arm's length most people other than my immediate family and Callie (who has been my best friend since childhood). I try not to let people close if being nice makes them want to come nearer so instead I am often cold; civil, polite but cold.

"But why, AMELIA? I don't understand. You're such an attractive individual when you let yourself be. Why don't you want people to like you?" I asked.

"I don't view liking me as something to avoid; rather, being cold and civil results in most people disliking you as an inevitable side effect - and so I made peace with this outcome, though liking me wasn't exactly my aim," AMELIA noted.

"So, what is your end goal?" I questioned in disbelief.

"I don't want anyone too close, as I don't want to become dependent on anyone and love anyone enough for their absence to affect me too greatly," she stated.

"Oh AMELIA," I asked. "Doesn't that seem incredibly lonely?"

She shrugged her shoulders.

"Yes, but I prefer my life with her better," she concluded.

"Do you not care about having friends and people to rely on?" I pushed her further.

"No," she replied with an obvious shrug and continued talking without my having to push her further. "Several years ago, I thought I had met my perfect person - my soul mate or whatever you wish to call them - who made my life truly blissful; everything about the relationship seemed amazing but looking back now I should have realized it was too good to be true."

She stopped suddenly and I saw tears welling in her eyes, which began to concern me since this wasn't meant to upset her and now that I had asked, this discussion seemed more awkward than before.

"He was my whole world until he died in a car accident, and the pain has never subsided since. To this day, I don't know how I survived; yet one way that would ensure this never happens again would be not getting close enough with anyone to care either way about them," she stated.

I moved over and took her hand in mine, gently squeezing it.

"AMELIA," I replied in sorrowful tones. "I can only imagine what that must have been like for you at such an early age.

She sniffled, tried to smile but her bottom lip wobbled slightly, picked up her drink, took a large gulp from it to attempt to mask her discomfort; but this didn't work; I could feel her anguish as though written on the air between us.

"Please forgive my being bold in asking this, but are you sure this is a healthy way of dealing with your grief? Have you considered therapy as an option?" I asked.

AMELIA laughed then, and my anxiety eased slightly. Though she appeared upset beneath the laughter, she wasn't looking quite as devastated.

"I thought I was handling things the best way possible and for a time it worked well for me; however, that may no longer be the case," she replied. I asked why.

She gave me another sorrowful smile.

"Because I met someone who managed to overcome the wall," she explained.

As she spoke, a thick tear fell from her eye. I quickly reached up and used my thumb to wipe it away from her cheek. As soon as my touch touched her cheek, we both looked back at each other before our lips connected in kissing each other passionately.
Though our kiss was deeply passionate and full of emotion, when it ended I could see AMELIA's surprise and recognize it all over her face.

"No," I stated firmly and my voice dropped into an audible whisper.

She didn't reply; instead she stood up, took my hand, and led me back into our room. Something told me I wouldn't be spending the night sitting on that sofa.

AMELIA

Craig died and took part of me with him; what remained behind was red, raw, and gaping open, leaving a trail of pain in its wake. It affected every nerve of my body.

I felt trapped, not knowing whether I would perish but also not having hope of rescue.

Over time, my heartache over missing Craig had become easier to bear; yet still I was careful never to open up to anyone new. RON was one person I thought didn't warrant much concern because I didn't like him at first glance - well that turned out to be false as somehow, I let this bastard in and felt terrified yet excited at once; my head wasn't making sense anymore either!

That was why, when RON told me he wouldn't go anywhere, I didn't respond immediately with words of my own; that was the best possible response I could offer, yet verbal communication wasn't possible between us; what was important was feeling his presence close by: his heart beating against my chest and feeling him inside of me - becoming one with him as we became one and let our feelings merge; something RON hadn't said directly but somehow knew: for us both to let go and become one again - let him and let go so that any remaining tension between us would dissipate; that would allow us to break free.

As each brick crumbled away, I needed to release myself of any remaining pain or distress I was still holding onto.

As soon as I entered our hotel room, I immediately started taking off my clothes. Nodding to RON for him to do the same, he soon followed suit within less than one minute and we stood and faced each other completely undress; within moments of doing this I was gasping for breath from what RON was causing me, his chest rising and falling more frequently than usual suggesting this could also be happening to him.

As my eyes traveled over his body, taking in his muscular chest, gorgeous abs and large cock. Finally unable to wait any longer for him inside me, I closed the gap between us by wrapping my arms around RON's shoulders before pulling him closer for kisses while his arm wrapped itself around my waist.

He ran his hands down my body, cupped my ass and lifted me off of the ground. As his hands roamed back up my body again, my legs wrapped themselves around his waist while our tongues collided as we explored each other's mouths.

As RON and I kissed, he headed towards the bathroom. I assumed he wanted us to share a bath or shower; instead he kicked shut the bathroom door while we were still in our bedroom and pressed himself against me hard - an intense sensation of fire engulfing every part of me as RON's warmth and power enveloped every part of my body.

He held me in place with his body, running his hands along my arms until they held mine in his. Then he lifted my arms above my head, grasping both wrists in one of his hands, holding them there.

He eased my feet back onto the floor and used his free hand to push apart my thighs. I side stepped eagerly with one foot to give him all of the access he required; as his fingers ran from my pussy to my clit, leaving a trail of juices as they did so.
He arrived and I was already wet as could be when he arrived; his gentle yet playful touch only added more moisture into my system.

He smiled as I groaned my frustrations, then leaned his head toward mine - without kissing, instead running his tongue lightly over my lips - only for him not to give in and instead leave me longing for more; just bringing me onto the edge and leaving me hanging - leaving me wanting more and wanting more from him.

I struggled to move against his fingers, pressing against them to press my clit against them but they moved away instead of pressing against me. When I begged them for touch they smiled again but only gave a light, teaseful touch again; my hands tried to break free but were held tightly enough against my will that it couldn't happen.

Accepting my situation was the key to having fun on this ride, so I closed my eyes before opening them when he bit my nipple and breathed through my teeth as the two sensations compounded each other to drive me madder than ever.

As RON seemed to sense I could no longer handle his continued pressure, he began rubbing my clit faster and with greater pressure, prompting me to moan. Instead of pulling his fingers away when I began writhing against his hand this time, RON instead pushed them through my slit, penetrating my pussy, leaving his thumb free to tend to my clit's needs while continuously moving his fingers in and out, rubbing over my g spot each time his hand moved into contact with me.

I could feel my stomach and clit begin to tighten as a result of both stimulations; RON seemed intent on taunting me further until my release was provided by some way or another.

I felt him begin to pull away, but I wasn't about to let that happen - not this time! If he were allowed, it could drive me insane and make me insane as well.

As I found no relief quickly, I began clamping my thighs together tightly, trapping his hand, while moving my hips so my clit was rubbing over his thumb. Squatting down ever so slightly for increased pressure on my clit was another tactic I employed but RON simply let it happen without ever stopping me.

I glanced over at him and noticed his mouth slightly open; when my gaze met his, he smiled warmly at me and winked when we made eye contact.

"You are truly incredible," he replied, and suddenly I stopped fighting him.

My climax came when RON continued pressing his thumb against my clit, harder and faster, until my climax struck me like an earthquake. As every nerve in my body throbbed to life and my skin tingled and pulsed with excitement, every muscle tightened, pussy clenched tighter, stomach contracted further... It felt as if all my cells had become one giant nerve ending that was overwhelmed with pleasure; just when I thought that wasn't possible anymore another wave came crashing over me, and my juices flooded RON's hand and my thighs with pleasure...

My body shook as I fell hard. My eyes began rolling back in my head as the pleasure overtook me and my vision turned red with every movement of RON against my body, matching how my muscles felt as they tightened with each stroke against mine. For an instant I floated in bliss until my eyes rolled back down again and all was normal and red had vanished, leaving RON back in my line of vision as all my muscles turned to shaking jelly-like substance. If not for RON against mine all might have collapsed onto the ground- I knew this moment would never have happened- it would have taken just one hit to have turned back to normal before coming against RON that made him turn as soon as it happened - or would it?

RON stopped me from falling, yet gave no respite. When my arms fell to his shoulders and then released again across his shoulders, RON lifted me up again, pushing himself inside of me until my still-throbbing g spot became tender to the touch. "Cry out!" as RON filled me up again until my body collapsed under him - this time around.

As RON continued his assault, I slowly found my balance again as I moved in time with his rhythm. Each movement seemed to encourage his attacks further as his breathing became increasingly irregular as he tried to prevent himself from orgasming.

He gave up, pressing me against the door as he burst inside of me. My body went stiff as his muscles tightened around my pussy and his name came whispered into my ear with its hint of seduction; sending chills through me. I held tight to him until his body went rigid with pained moaning followed by relaxing as he eased out of me onto a bed; pulling back its duvet then placing me there while lifting up its edge with questioning looks on both sides and raising eyebrows on each side!

"I think that should be fine," I replied with a laugh.

He slipped onto my bed beside me, and I rolled to face him. We lay there close, our arms around each other's bodies as we gazed into each other's eyes.

"Do you have any regrets?" RON inquired.

"No regrets," I promised myself. Two weeks later, as I headed towards the store to purchase groceries for dinner, my plan was to wait at RON's office until he finished work before heading over there myself to grab anything I might need for later that evening.

I didn't mind walking to the store - in fact I enjoyed it - but hated carrying all those groceries back.

I was stunned to find myself already missing RON after only two weeks of dating him, seeing each other almost every night of our short relationship. Last night was an exception due to a conference call in another time zone that kept him at work until midnight; even one night without seeing him had me missing him so badly already! That thought should have scared me, yet instead it left me excited! Something special could be beginning here and even with occasional pangs of guilt from losing Craig behind it was clear this was indeed time for something new and fresh to blossom.

I strolled into the store deliberating what to make for dinner when I stopped at an ATM to check my balance, knowing this would determine to some extent my spending options. Although still unemployed, an offer had come my way from one company that I was seriously considering taking up.

My jaw dropped when I saw my balance. What was happening? Surely the bank must have made some sort of error? So, I checked through my list of transactions to determine how much was actually missing from there compared to what was supposed to be there? After pressing some buttons and getting up a mini statement of account, my shock quickly transformed to anger.

My balance was accurate. RON had paid me for attending his sister's wedding event for one week. As soon as I hit the button to return my card, I rushed from the store without our dinner having taken place - instead marching directly up RON's building to his floor, down its corridors and directly into his office without bothering to knock before going in - telling anyone and everyone what had just transpired in no uncertain terms.

RON looked up from his desk when I opened the office door. He smiled briefly before stopping when he saw my expression; even then when I wanted to throttle him I couldn't help admiring how beautiful he was; yet that wouldn't derail me from what was important: getting work done.

"What am I talking about RON?" I said. His eyes appeared bewildered at my question about fees for wedding ceremonies. "Have we agreed upon a price?" he was surprised that I brought it up at all. "Does this include wedding insurance?" I queried.

"Oh no. Hasn't the item cleared yet? Sorry I thought escrow would have cleared today," she replied. "Let me call the bank."

"No!" I exclaimed. "I can't believe you treated me like some sort of prostitute.

"No, AMELIA. Please understand I didn't mean for it to appear that way at all; it just felt wrong for me not to send it and take advantage of our agreement, like I'd be taking advantage of you," RON replied.

"Don't take that bait!" I shouted at RON.

"Does it? As far as I'm concerned, from where I stand it's exactly the same... you were being paid to perform your service..."

He was still talking, but I could no longer hear him. Instead, the most intense pain ever to have arisen in my body suddenly tore through me as though someone were holding on tightly with a glove covered in broken glass fragments; all I could manage was a weak whimper of protest.

Oh no! I was going to die, and my last conversation with RON would likely have been a trivial disagreement over something which wasn't important in the grand scheme of things.

Another wave of pain wracked my body and tears streamed down my face as I wailed in agony.

"AMELIA? What's wrong?" was what RON was asking her.

RON's voice seemed to come from all around me rather than near me, yet when I tried to reply I couldn't speak - my eyes went blank as everything faded to black before RON caught me before I hit the floor and held me close in his arms. Before long everything became blurry again - then everything just vanished into nothingness.

RON

Iran left her office and I picked AMELIA up. Although I considered calling 911, I felt certain I could get her to the nearest hospital faster by myself.

I knew she needed medical help immediately, and had to get there quickly before the ambulance could arrive. Although I didn't understand exactly what was ailing her, I knew one thing - I simply could not lose her!

As I rode down in the elevator, muttering incoherently to it to hurry up, I immediately bolted across the foyer when it doors opened. One of the night security guards called out after me asking if everything was okay; rather than stop running or even slow down to answer him, I shouted no and continued running to my car where I unlocked and laid AMELIA down on its back seat before quickly unlatching and opening both back doors before wrenching open both front doors to leave with a squeal of tires before fleeing with one last squeal of tires before taking off into the night air.

As I left the parking lot, I made sure to drive cautiously. Driving too quickly could cause AMELIA to slip out from under me or could result in being pulled over and taking up valuable time; otherwise I might endanger AMELIA or myself in some other way.

Losing control and striking a lamp post would have killed us both instantly. So I drove at a few miles an hour over the speed limit; not quite late but not quite early either, with relatively quiet roads making it slightly easier for me to move quickly compared to a few hours earlier, although traffic still hindered progress significantly. Had an ambulance come sooner it would have had its advantages, with its sirens sounding and drivers moving aside as soon as AMELIA needed medical care; moreover, paramedics may already been treating AMELIA upon her arrival at our scene.

After what seemed like an eternity but was only five minutes or less, I finally saw the hospital up ahead. Once it came into view, I couldn't resist speeding up; taking two wheels onto hospital grounds to speed around corners until arriving at ER entrance and throwing car into park before quickly running back out and scooping AMELIA from behind seat without stopping to close doors before running into ER.

As I ran in, I asked for help and several people in the waiting room looked up in disapproval before eventually looking away again.

Looking away quickly, they seemed relieved that my emergency was not their concern. By then, however, the triage nurse who had been standing at reception desk had already hit the alarm, running towards me quickly to help.

She wanted to know what had occurred. "What happened?" was her question.

"I don't really know," I replied. "She seemed fine at first and then suddenly, in just moments, was doubled over in pain unable to speak out about it; after which, she just collapsed."

As soon as I explained the situation to the triage nurse, a doctor, two nurses, and someone with a trolley appeared beside me and heard what I had to say. AMELIA was placed onto the trolley immediately and instantly wheeled away; I attempted to follow them but one of the nurses blocked my path.

"Sir," she advised him.

"But," I began, before she interjected: "Please sir, the more time I spend debating with you is less time I get to spend with your wife.

I decided not to correct her; instead I just nodded and nodded away. The nurse quickly left, while I left to move my car outside. While calling AMELIA's mom might cause further anxiety for both of us, calling would only serve to further distress her in my estimation and I had no definitive information I could offer her anyway.

After running inside, leaving my keys in the ignition with all doors wide open and keys in place - I was somewhat amazed that my car had still been left there in the parking lot when I returned out again and left its doors wide open with both keys still in the ignition - something must have gone right this evening - I jogged back out into the waiting room of ER room where they let me sit down.

Just moments after I sat down, the nurse who had stopped me from following AMELIA appeared in the waiting room. She signaled for me to follow her into an adjacent private room where she gestured for me to sit down.

"Is she alright?" I asked the nurse. The doctor has advised that you go directly to the surgical ward because that's where she will go after her procedure and where you can speak directly with the surgeon," the nurse replied. You may remain here as long as necessary in the meantime.

Once AMELIA had left, I took a minute and sat quietly, clutching my face between my hands. Why had this happened to AMELIA when she seemed young and healthy? Speculating was only making my fears stronger; all I knew for certain was that AMELIA must be okay; losing her would be unbearable.

My time with her had made me realize that I never wanted to part ways with her again. I had fallen completely and hopelessly in love with a woman whom just three short weeks prior I would have described as one I despised with great fervor.

AMELIA

I awoke slowly, like someone treading water. The last time I'd felt as deeply asleep was the morning after RON and I had our first sexual experience together.

But this night was different. My stomach hurt, and there was an alarm clock beeping nearby. Reaching to turn it off didn't work - eventually opening my eyes made things clearer.

As I took in the white ceiling and walls, sterile-looking blue blanket, and white and blue-spotted gown that covered me, it became apparent to me that I was indeed in hospital. Why had they brought me here?

"When I attempted to sit up, a sharp pain shot through my stomach. As soon as the discomfort subsided, I dropped back down again with an audible grunt."

"Darling, please wait a bit," RON advised his client.

"He was still here. Even after my yelling had angered him, he remained. Tears began streaming down my cheeks."

"Are you experiencing pain?" RON inquired with care in his voice.

"No," I replied in a low whisper, "That isn't why I'm crying." And you stayed, too? He asked.

mes

I explained. "I overreacted, said something unkind and you didn't leave." Eventually I burst out crying again as soon as we parted ways for good. I told myself it wouldn't happen again: but you were there despite it all and stood there while I overreacted even more - that caused this whole incident."

"Of course I stayed," RON answered with a slight laugh, "and it will take more than that for me to leave this place.

"Good to know!" I joked, and we both laughed before my stomach suddenly tightened with discomfort. I winced in pain before turning around in confusion to ask: "What happened?"

"I don't know. The nurse advised us just to wait here with you and that the surgeon would soon arrive," said he.

"Had surgery?" I inquired. RON replied that they thought I knew. They don't understand why though."

I pushed the bell for a nurse. I needed answers on why this was happening to me and she came a few minutes later with a warm smile on her face.

"Well, you seem to have come around. Let me get Doctor Patterson over to speak to you," the woman replied.

After she left before I could ask any questions, I hoped Doctor Patterson wouldn't pull a similar stunt. Within minutes he entered, looking more youthful than expected for an surgeon; with blonde floppy hair, blue eyes, and an impressively large nose.

"Greetings Ms Rogers", he replied with a warm smile.

"Call me AMELIA," I murmured. "How do you know my name anyway?"

RON said, "I informed them."

Oh yes. Clearly the anesthetic must have rendered me somewhat dozy, I thought to myself.

"How are you feeling?" Doctor Patterson inquired.

"Overall," I replied.

He commented, "That's great," noting how tenuous things had been prior to. Your appendix had burst, and in two to three more minutes you may have gone into septic shock, with significant complications likely arising for both of them. We likely would have lost you.

"That was quite something," I replied as I stopped for a second to take it all in, yet Doctor Patterson wasn't done unleashing her bombs yet.

"Don't worry. There is no reason for you not to make a swift and complete recovery, and your baby should be fine," according to him.

"Oh no," I asked in surprise. The doctor replied that I hadn't known because it was still so early. When you're ready to leave here, arrange an appointment with your regular OB-GYN and start thinking about finding an OB-GYN as soon as possible."

"No, I think you must have me confused with someone else. I am not pregnant; instead I am taking birth control."

"Ms... AMELIA, it is no secret that you are pregnant despite birth control being less-than-effective. Please excuse me, as I must leave for surgery in half an hour," Doctor Patterson replied before disappearing without answering my many questions.

As I took a deep breath and considered how pregnant was making me feel, my stomach started churning with excitement and I began smiling knowingly at being expecting one for once in my life - something I never expected when we first began dating less than month before! Knowing RON wouldn't agree, I turned my head towards him before breaking my silence about my unhappiness with being pregnant.

"RON, you do not have to be part of this," I replied. "I won't hold it against you; we haven't been together long and..."

He reached out and gently placed his fingers against my lips as an attempt to silence me, prompting me to stop talking and stare into his eyes. I stopped my own voice from speaking further.

"Yes, you did try harder to rid yourself of me this time around." "Yes, indeed. You did put forth extra effort.
"AMELIA, I have told you I won't leave. Don't think that my staying is only because you are pregnant - while the idea of becoming a father certainly excites me greatly - but instead because I love you," he replied.

Tears welled up in my eyes and I blinked them away quickly before pushing past the lump that had suddenly formed in my throat.

"I love you too," I whispered softly.

At that moment, despite being hospitalized and having just undergone surgery, everything seemed right with my world.

EPILOGUE - RON: Ten Months Later My grandmother smiled down upon the baby and looked up to AMELIA and me with pride, before looking down upon RON again to give us another hug and smiled warmly at us all.

"She is absolutely adorable," the staff confirmed, "and quite beautiful as well. Are you certain about the name?"

AMELIA can't think of anyone else she would rather Evelyn be named after; Evelyn is such an elegant name!

My grandmother smiled broadly before looking down at my newborn niece.

"And to think, when I first met your mom and your father they were playing some silly game where they pretended to date despite not really liking each other - possibly to make an older lady happy - but now all is well; they realized it wasn't all an act and are both happy indeed!"

"What!" I exploded, shocked. "Hadn't you known all along?"

"Of course I did Raf. I'm old but not stupid. No one else noticed, but that's because they don't recognize what's right there," she replied. When questioned by me why she hadn't spoken up earlier. She responded by explaining her inaction. I asked why nobody had mentioned anything either before.

"Because I could see that something was developing between you two, and had I told them the game was over, they may never have continued spending time together - thus leading to this little girl," my grandmother explained.

At first I was surprised, though now it seems foolish of me. If there was anyone who understood what was really going on it was her.

AMELIA and I shared lunch with my grandmother while baby Evelyn napped; afterward, we took a stroll down the street outside my grandmother's home.

"Remember our deal?" I asked him. If my grandmother detects anything amiss with our deal, the deal is off - therefore, I believe you owe me an amount substantial amount.

"Nope. Sorry buddy - someone convinced me to use the money for buying my own daycare center," AMELIA replied, nudging me and smiling knowingly.

"That was good advice," I laughed. "However, in regards to your debt: there may be other ways." AMELIA gave a playful slap across my arm as we laughed together; we both wrapped an arm around one another before she cuddled against me - and for one moment only, my world felt complete and secure.

Perfect. Perfectly.

THE END

The edits and layout of this print version are Copyright © 2023 by Indrajeet Nayak

www.ingramcontent.com/pod-product-compliance
Lightning Source LLC
LaVergne TN
LVHW070539070526
838199LV00076B/6810

9789359803814